DIANA'S WHITE HOUSE GARDEN

Elisa Carbone

illustrated by Jen Hill

Viking

For Diana Hopkins Halsted, with many thanks for sharing her stories with me, and for my grandson, Alexander Mark Miskolczi —**E.C.**

For Little Bee, my faithful intern —**J.H.**

Viking

Penguin Young Readers Group

An imprint of Penguin Random House LLC

375 Hudson Street

New York, New York 10014

First published in the United States of America by Viking,

an imprint of Penguin Random House LLC, 2016

LIBRARY OF CONGRESS CATALOGING-IN-PUBLICATION DATA IS AVAILABLE

ISBN: 978-0-670-01649-5

1 3 5 7 9 10 8 6 4 2

Manufactured in China   Book design by Nancy Brennan   Set in Eames Century Modern

This art was created using pencil, gouache, and digital.

Diana Hopkins lived in a white house.

The White House.

She lived there with her father, Harry Hopkins, who was the president's chief advisor; and the housekeepers and butlers; and George, the groundskeeper; and of course President Roosevelt and his wife, Eleanor.

It was 1943, and the White House was a busy place.

The United States was at war. American soldiers were fighting across the world.

"We all need to do our part to win this war," President Roosevelt said.

Diana *wanted* to do her part. But what could a ten-year-old girl do?

"I could be a spy!" Diana decided. To practice, she snuck into the dumbwaiter and rode it down to the White House basement kitchen. Then she tried to tiptoe away without anyone seeing her.

But Mrs. Nesbitt, the head housekeeper, caught her. "The dumbwaiter is for dirty linen, not little girls," she said sternly.

The next day, Diana played with Fala, the
Roosevelts' little Scottish terrier.
They played catch.

And fetch the stick.

Fala ran after Diana as she roller-
skated on the driveway past the White
House guards.

Then they sat together and rested.

"I know, Fala," Diana said. "I could be a city official—those are the people who hang important signs, like AIR-RAID SHELTER or BUY WAR BONDS."

To practice, she painted a very important sign. But where to hang it?

On the second floor she peeked into her father's study. He was working quietly at his desk.

Just as quietly, Diana lifted up the sign and hung it outside his door. QUARANTINE. MEASLES. KEEP OUT!

At supper, her father sighed. "What if the president needed me, but my office said KEEP OUT?" he asked her.

Diana promised not to hang any more signs.

But she still wanted to help with the war effort.

She decided to listen to one of President Roosevelt's Fireside Chats on the radio. "My fellow Americans . . ." he began, and then he talked about how citizens and soldiers needed to work together to defeat the enemy.

What if enemies tried to come to the White House? Diana wondered. How could they be kept away? She had an idea.

She put pins in all the satin chairs in the Red Room, the Green Room, and the Blue Room.
Sharp pins, sticking straight up. That would send enemies away in a hurry.

The housekeepers found the pins and took them out just in time for Eleanor
Roosevelt's formal afternoon tea. They found *most* of the pins, anyway.

"Ouch!"

Mrs. Roosevelt's friend was not happy.

Mrs. Roosevelt was not happy.

Diana got sent to her room.

One evening Diana went to the Oval Office, where her father was chatting with President Roosevelt. She stood near the president's chair and played with the toys on his desk. There were little carved donkeys and elephants, and a teddy bear named Uncle Teddy.

"Harry, I've decided I want most of the food our farmers grow to go right to our soldiers, to make sure they're well fed and strong," the president said to Diana's father.

Mr. Hopkins frowned. "But then what will our civilians eat?" he asked.

"I have a plan," said President Roosevelt. "I want people to grow their own food."

Mr. Hopkins raised his eyebrows.

The president continued. "I want every backyard and vacant lot turned into a garden. That way, our soldiers *and* our citizens will be well fed and strong. We'll call them Victory Gardens, because they will help us win the war."

Diana's father nodded. "An excellent idea, Mr. President."

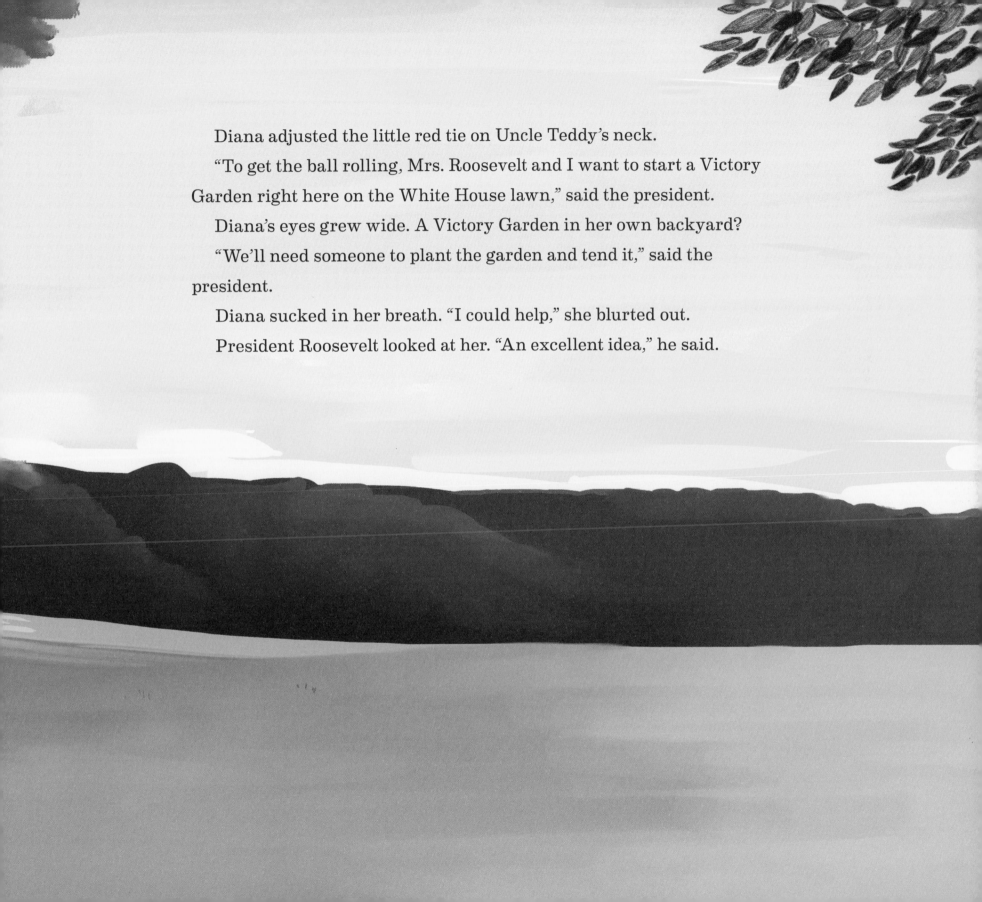

Diana adjusted the little red tie on Uncle Teddy's neck.

"To get the ball rolling, Mrs. Roosevelt and I want to start a Victory Garden right here on the White House lawn," said the president.

Diana's eyes grew wide. A Victory Garden in her own backyard?

"We'll need someone to plant the garden and tend it," said the president.

Diana sucked in her breath. "I could help," she blurted out.

President Roosevelt looked at her. "An excellent idea," he said.

Diana's father bought her a pair of overalls so she could get to work right away. Mrs. Roosevelt chose a spot on the South Lawn right next to the driveway, where there was lots of sunshine.

Diana worked with George, the
groundskeeper.

They turned over the soil.

They fertilized with chicken manure.

Then Diana planted bean seeds
and carrot seeds, cabbage plants and
tomato plants.

She went to her garden each morning before school.

On Monday, Mrs. Roosevelt showed her how to water.

On Tuesday, George taught her how to weed.

On Wednesday, she watered all by herself.

Soon the beans and carrots sprouted, and tiny green tomatoes appeared on the tomato plants.

One morning Diana stepped out onto the White House lawn. The sun shone brightly and dew sparkled on the boxwoods and magnolia trees. Everything was beautiful and alive. She went to see her garden.

But what she saw shocked her.

Half of her seedlings were *gone*!

Diana gasped. She leaned over to inspect the tiny stubs. Then she heard a rustling.

Rabbits!

Diana scowled. If she couldn't get this garden to grow, she might never find a way to help with the war effort.

She wagged one finger at Fala. "*Your* job," she said, "is to keep those rabbits out of my Victory Garden!"

Then she stomped inside to breakfast.

Eleanor Roosevelt helped Diana replant. "Sometimes you just have to start over," said Mrs. Roosevelt cheerfully.

Soon the new seedlings came up healthy and strong. Diana kept them watered and weeded. The tomatoes were getting bigger, but none of them was ripe yet. Diana wondered when there would be something to harvest.

"Fala, gardens sure do take a lot of waiting," she said.

Fala kept a watchful eye on the garden.

He chased those rabbits all the way to Pennsylvania Avenue.

One day, Mrs. Roosevelt told Diana to dress in her overalls, brush her hair, and meet her in the garden. Diana did as she was told, but when she got to the garden, there were two strangers with Mrs. Roosevelt, a man and a woman.

"Ah, the little girl who is inspiring the whole country!" the woman said, and she reached out to shake Diana's hand. Then she lifted her camera and began to take pictures.

"How does it feel to be helping with the war effort?" the man asked. He held a pad
of paper and a pencil, ready to write down her answer.

Diana straightened up tall. "It feels very good," she said.

She only wished that there was something to *eat* in the garden for the woman to
take pictures of.

A few days later, her father brought her a newspaper. "You're getting famous!" he said. There was a picture of *her*, dressed in overalls, hoeing her garden. "Diana Farms Her White House Plot" the headline read.

The article went on to say how all across America people were plowing up city parks and vacant lots, backyards and even front yards, and planting fruits and vegetables. President Roosevelt's plan was working! And she was an important part of it.

One morning, as Diana walked toward her garden something caught her eye—something red.

What could it be?

She went closer.

The tomatoes were . . . finally ripe!

But that wasn't all. Beans hung like slender fingers, and carrots pushed their orange shoulders out of the ground. Diana ran inside to find Mrs. Roosevelt. "Are they ready to *eat*?" she asked.

Mrs. Roosevelt came to see. She smiled. "Yes, Diana, take a basket and harvest our supper. Cut the biggest cabbage, too. We'll have a feast."

That evening, the White House cook made a wonderful supper:
beef stew with carrots and green beans, cabbage salad,
and sliced tomatoes. Everyone cleaned their plates.

"Diana, you've done a fine job," said President Roosevelt. "And not just in your own backyard, but for the whole country."

After supper Diana went outside to her garden. Fireflies flickered on and off.
She patted Fala on the head.

"You know what?" she asked Fala. "We *both* did a fine job."

AUTHOR'S NOTE

The World War II Victory Garden plan grew out of necessity. There was not enough steel and tin to make both fighter planes and tin cans for vegetables. There were not enough train cars to carry soldiers to the ports and to send food around the country. And with Japan controlling the islands where most of the world's rubber plants grew, there was not enough rubber for tires for trucks to carry food from the farms to the cities.

The Roosevelts' plan was a resounding success. In every city and town, vacant land was turned to food production. City parks, suburban and urban yards, vacant lots, and even apartment rooftops were used to grow fruits and vegetables. An estimated 20 million gardens were planted in the U.S., producing between 9 and 10 million tons of food, over 40 percent of all the produce eaten in the United States. Community centers offered classes in canning, and the harvest was put away to feed the country during the winter as well.

Diana Hopkins (now Diana Halsted) fondly remembers her time as the White House victory gardener, and how her story reached the country via the newspaper and magazine articles written about her. She also remembers playing with Fala, riding the dumbwaiter, hanging the MEASLES sign outside her father's door, and putting pins in all those chairs, and the trouble she got into when one of Mrs. Roosevelt's friends sat on one!

Diana continued to have a vegetable garden as she grew up and became an adult, and she now grows tomatoes, string beans, and zucchini in her backyard garden in Virginia.

ILLUSTRATOR'S NOTE

A lot of research went into depicting Diana's world. Thanks to the New York Public Library, the FDR Library and Museum in Hyde Park, N.Y., the PBS miniseries *The Roosevelts: An Intimate History*, and countless Internet references, I was able to portray details with historical accuracy.

When the events in this story took place in 1943, the world was very different than it is today. Segregation was still legal. However, Eleanor Roosevelt, a staunch advocate for civil rights, insisted that the White House domestic staff be African American. The butler shown in the second spread is John Pye, famed for having purchased the very first War Bond from President Roosevelt in 1942.

The first official Wonder Woman comic debuted in the summer of 1942—just in time for Diana to realistically be reading it. I found it a fun prop as well as an apt metaphor for Diana's determination to be a hero to her country.

I hope you are as delighted and inspired by Diana Hopkins as I was.

Diana Hopkins with First Lady Eleanor Roosevelt on the South Lawn, 1939.